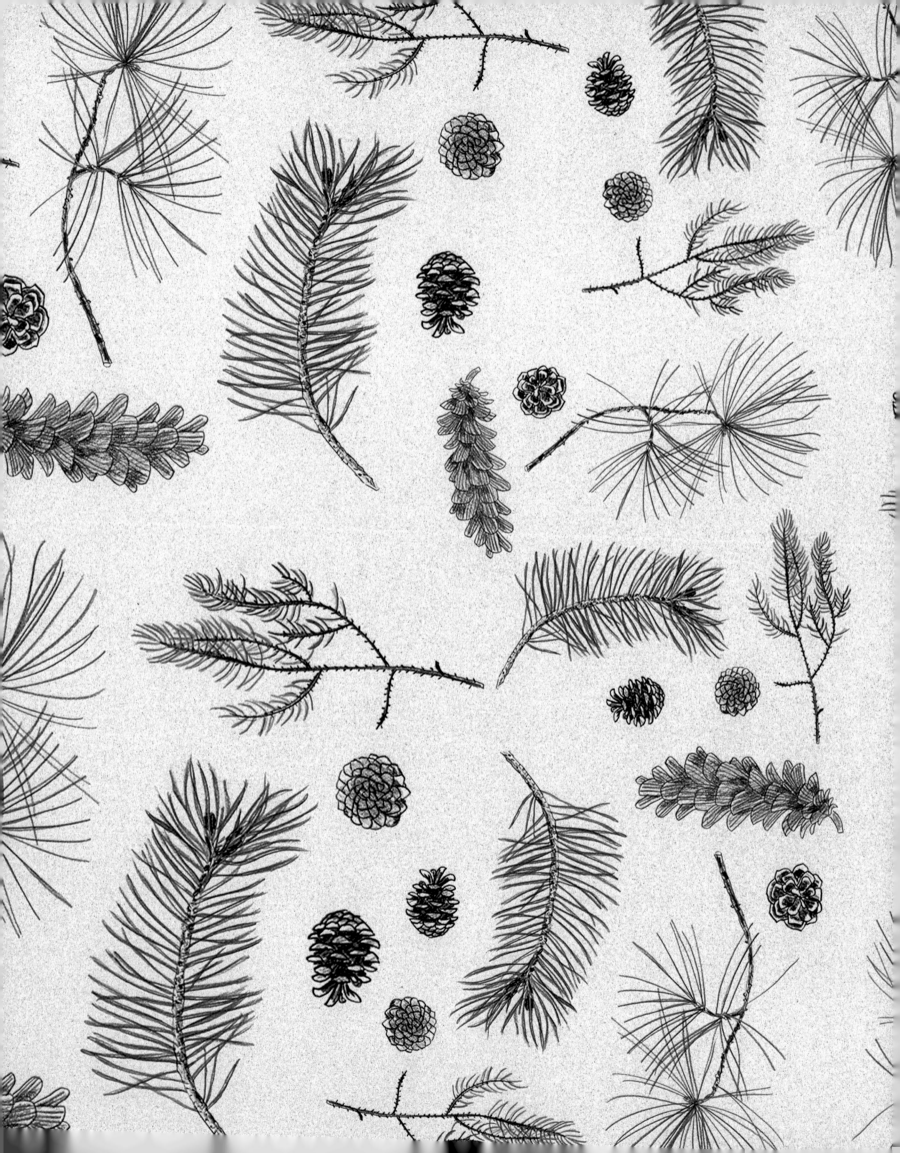

A Porcupine's Promenade

AN ENCOUNTER IN THE WINTER WOODS

BY

Lyn Smith

ILLUSTRATED BY

Jamie Hogan

MAINE AUTHORS PUBLISHING

2016

A PORCUPINE'S PROMENADE
An encounter in the winter woods

©2016 Lyn Smith

ISBN: 978-1-63381-091-4

illustrations ©2016 Jamie Hogan

designed and produced by

Maine Authors Publishing
12 High Street, Thomaston, Maine 04861
www.maineauthorspublishing.com

Printed in the United States of America

Stay Wild

Sam M Smith (signature)

To B, E, K, & N—my prickle of explorers.

—Lyn Smith

To my prickle on Peaks with love.

—Jamie Hogan

R ight outside my front door is an ice-cold winter playground.
"Mom," I shout. "Have you seen my snowshoes?"
"I'm going out for a walk in the woods."

Pflump, Pflump, Pflump.

My snowshoes push the deep snow down under my feet.
The forest is cold in the morning.
My hands are warm in my gloves.

The sun is bright and shines through the branches of the tall
evergreen trees.

I see my shadow.

I move quietly.

In front of me I see a big hemlock tree with patches of granite rocks circling the large trunk.

A dark hollow has been dug between the roots.

Who dug this hole?

I am curious and bend low to peek into the darkness.

Who is in there?

Two bright eyes shine out at me!
I know who it is.

Look!

It's a porcupine!
"Good morning," I whisper.

The porcupine twitches her brown nose at me and burrows
deeper in the hole.
I shuffle backwards because I know what can happen when
a porcupine is startled.

Do you?

I quietly watch as she begins to creep out of the hole.

The top of her small head is covered in black fur.
Her cheeks are covered in tiny milk-white quills.
Thousands of longer quills protect her furry round back
and flat tail. The claws on her toes are pointed and sharp.

I murmur, "You are a prickly porcupine.
          I think I will call you Priscilla."

Priscilla snuffles.
She grunts.

She waddles out onto a well-worn path in the snow, first down into the valley between the snowdrifts, and then up over the frozen hills of ice.

I can't help smiling as I watch her coat of quills swing back and forth with each step.
I decide to follow her.

    Whoosh, Whoosh, Whoosh.

Priscilla hears my snowshoes behind her.

Instantly she stops, turns, and stamps her feet at me.

She chatters and clacks her teeth.

Tchic - ttt - Tchik - ttt - Tchic - ttt - Tchick.

Her quills look as sharp as needles as they stand up straight
in the black fur on her back and tail.

I stop.
It would be a mistake to move any closer.
Priscilla's warning has worked.
She turns and moves on.

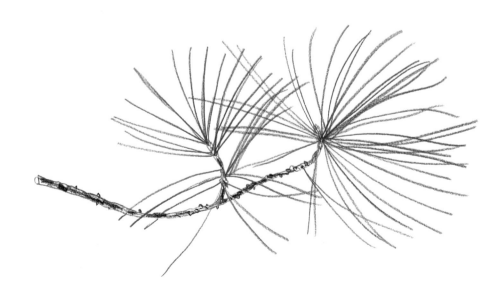

I wonder why Priscilla would leave the safety of her warm den to come out on this cold winter day?

She waddles around fallen pinecones and down the snowy trail to a pile of hemlock twigs scattered on the forest floor.

She uses her sharp teeth to tug the soft bark off the thick twigs.

Oh!

She's having a picnic!

When Priscilla is full, she looks around her.

What will she do next?

Priscilla moves forward in the snow on the trail
and turns her head from side to side.

The breeze rustles through the tree tops.

She stops at the bottom of a giant white-pine tree,
sniffs the cold air and rubs her muzzle against the tree.

Then she digs her long sharp claws into the trunk of the
pine tree and climbs.

Skrrrraaak…

Skrrrraaak…

Priscilla appears content and happy to be with her family.

Her eyes close on this peaceful sunny winter afternoon.

"Baaaiillleeey...."

Mom's voice echoes through the tops of the forest trees.
Time to return home.

My snowshoes backtrack along the trail.

I wonder....

Do porcupines dream?

Understanding and Caring for our Backyard Wildlife

Porcupines are North American mammals who are medium sized, quiet, and slow moving creatures with poor eyesight. However, these herbivores have a good sense of hearing and smell. Like other rodents, a porcupine has two large front teeth that grow continuously. The animal controls this growth by gnawing on the bark of coniferous trees. Protection from predators occurs when they demonstrate their agility by climbing trees. Porcupines have more than 30,000 quills, which cover most of their body. They have been described as looking like an "armored ball."

These quills are sharp barbed hollow spines and quickly release from a porcupines body when the animal is threatened. Porcupines do not hibernate; however, they stay in dens during inclement weather and winter. Dens are located in a hollow log or tree, a rock ledge, or under the stump of a tree. They are nocturnal but will forage for food during the day. Porcupines are the only mammal with antibiotics in their skin. This medicine prevents infection if a porcupine falls out of a tree and happens to be stuck with one of its own quills. Porcupines can live up to 30 years.

About the Author & Illustrator

©photo by Brian Smith

LYN SMITH holds a M.Ed. in Literacy and a Certificate of Advanced Study in Reading Education. She began her career as a kindergarten teacher and has since worked as an educational administrator and an adjunct faculty member at a local community college, as well as providing classroom reading/writing instructional supports as a literacy coach in Portland, Maine. She is currently an instructional strategist/reading specialist at Kennebunk Elementary School. Lyn divides her time between trail walks in the nearby nature preserves and the sandy beaches near her home.
To learn more about Lyn, visit: www.lyn-smith.com.

©photo by Peter Ralston

JAMIE HOGAN teaches illustration at Maine College of Art and is the award-winning illustrator of *Rickshaw Girl*, *A Warmer World*, and *Here Come the Humpbacks!* She grew up hiking and skiing in the White Mountains of New Hampshire, never once spying a porcupine, and now lives on an island off the coast of Maine with her husband and daughter.
To see more of her work, visit: www.jamiehogan.com.

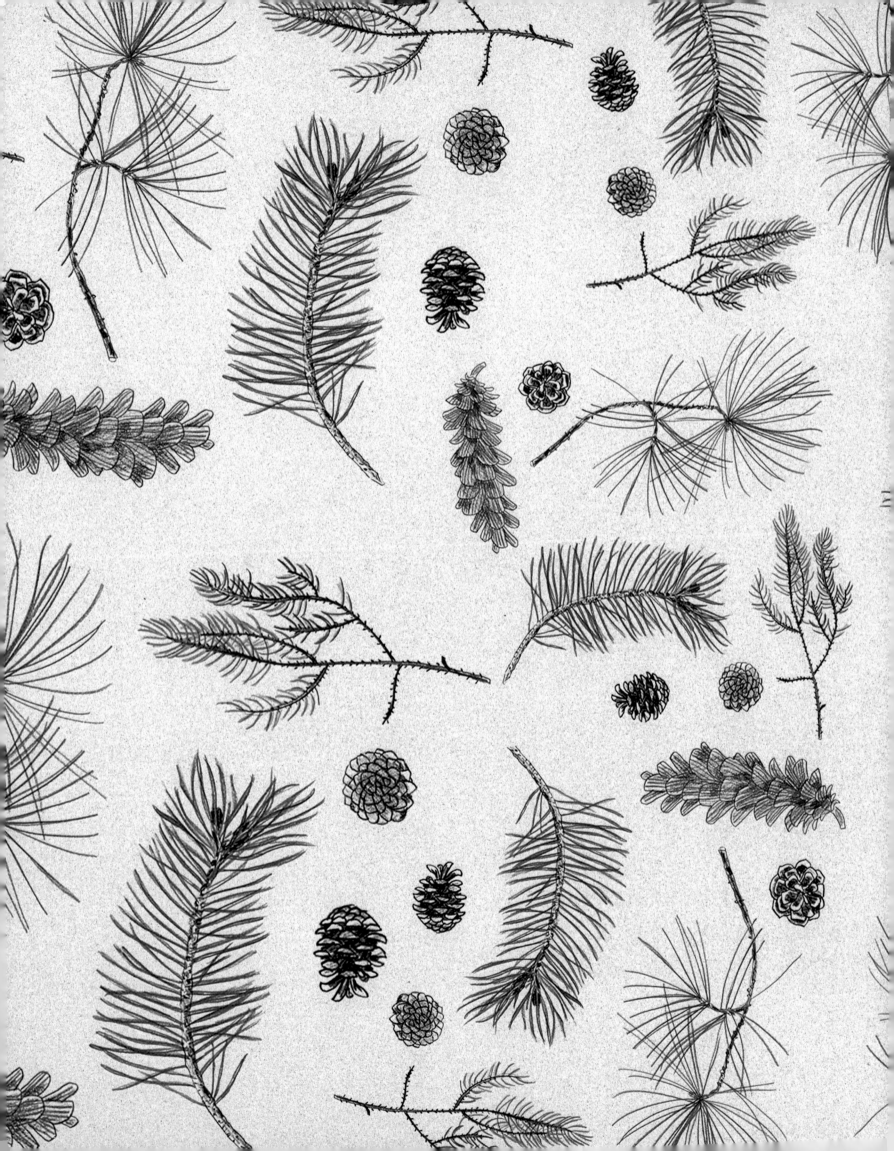